Princess
Mirror-Belle

Books by Julia Donaldson

★ JULIA DONALDSON ★
Princess Mirror-Belle

Illustrated by
✳ LYDIA MONKS ✳

MACMILLAN CHILDREN'S BOOKS

These stories first published 2003 in *Princess Mirror-Belle* by
Macmillan Children's Books

This edition published 2017 by Macmillan Children's Books
an imprint of Pan Macmillan
20 New Wharf Road, London N1 9RR
Associated companies throughout the world
www.panmacmillan.com

ISBN 978-1-5098-8022-5

1 3 5 7 9 8 6 4 2

A CIP catalogue record for this book is available from
the British Library.

Printed and bound by CPI Group (UK) Ltd, Croydon CR0 4YY

For Phoebe

Contents

Chapter One

Dragon Pox

"You've got some new ones on your face," said Ellen's mum. "Don't scratch them or you'll make them worse."

Ellen was off school with chicken pox. She didn't feel all that ill but she *did* feel sorry for herself, because she was missing the school outing to the dolphin display.

"Can you read me a story?" she asked Mum. But just then the front door bell rang.

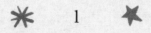

"I'm sorry, I can't. That's Mrs Foster-Smith come for her piano lesson. Look, here are your library books . . . and remember, *no scratching*." She went out of the room.

Ellen picked up one of the books. It was full of stories about princesses. She flicked through the pages, looking at the pictures. The princesses were all very beautiful, with swirly looking clothes and hair down to their waists. None of them had chicken pox. Ellen started to read *The Sleeping Beauty*, but it was difficult to concentrate. For one thing, her spots were so itchy. For another, Mrs Foster-Smith was thumping away at "The Fairies' Dance" on the piano downstairs. The way she played it, it sounded more like "The Elephants' Dance".

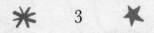

Ellen decided to have a look at her new spots. There was no mirror in her bedroom so she put on her right slipper (she had lost her left one) and padded into the bathroom.

She studied her face in the mirror over the basin. One of the new spots was right in the middle of her nose. The more Ellen looked at it, the itchier it felt . . . Her hand crept towards it. Just a little *tiny* scratch wouldn't matter, surely. Her finger was just about to touch the spot when a strange

thing happened. Her reflection dodged to one side and said, "Don't scratch or you'll turn into a toad!"

Ellen didn't reply. She was too surprised. She just stared.

"I've never *seen* such a bad case of dragon pox," said the mirror girl.

"It's not dragon pox, it's *chicken* pox," Ellen found herself saying. "Anyway, yours is just as bad – you're my reflection."

"Don't be silly, I'm not you," said the mirror girl, and to prove it she stuck one hand out of the mirror and then the other.

"Come on, help me out," she said,

reaching for Ellen's
hand.

Ellen gave a
gentle pull and the
mirror girl climbed out
of the mirror, into
the basin and down
on to the bathroom
floor.

"What a funny little room!" she said.

"It's not *that* little!" said Ellen. This was
true – there was room in the bathroom for
three of the tall pot plants that Mum was
so keen on.

The mirror girl laughed. "The bathroom
in the palace is about ten times this size,"
she said.

"The *palace*?" repeated Ellen.

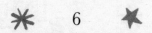

"Of course. Where would you expect a princess to live?"

"Are you a princess, then?"

"I most certainly am. I'm Princess Mirror-Belle. You really ought to curtsy, but as you're my friend I'll let you off."

"But . . . you don't *look* like a princess," said Ellen. "You look just like me. You've got the same pyjamas and just one slipper. You've even got a plaster on your finger like me."

"These are just my dressing-up clothes," said Mirror-Belle. "In the palace I usually wear a dress of silver silk, like the moon." She thought for a moment and then added, "Or one of golden satin, like the sun. And anyway, my slipper's on my *left* foot and my plaster's on my *right* finger. Yours are

the other way round."

Ellen didn't see that this made much difference, but she didn't want to get into an argument, so instead she asked Mirror-Belle, "Why have you got the plaster? Did you cut yourself on the bread knife like me?"

"No, of course not," said Mirror-Belle. "I was pricked on my finger by a wicked fairy."

"Just like the Sleeping Beauty!" said Ellen. "Did you go to sleep for a hundred years too?"

"No – two hundred," said Mirror-Belle. "I only woke up this morning." She gave a huge yawn as if to prove it.

"Did you put the plaster on before you went to sleep or after you woke up?" asked Ellen, but Mirror-Belle didn't seem to want to answer this question. Instead she put the plug into the bath and turned on the taps.

"Hey, what are you doing?" asked Ellen.

"Getting the cure ready, what do you think?"

"What cure?"

"The cure for dragon pox, of course."

"But I haven't got dragon pox!"

 9

"Well, I have," said Mirror-Belle, "and I'll tell you how I got it. I was in the palace garden last week, playing with my golden ball, when—"

"Weren't you still asleep last week?" Ellen interrupted. "Didn't you say you only woke up this morning?"

"I wish you'd stop asking so many questions. As I was about to say, an enormous dragon flew down and captured me. Luckily a knight came and rescued me, but when I got back to the palace I came out in all these spots. My mother the Queen sent for the doctor and he said I'd caught dragon pox."

"Well, my doctor said mine were chicken pox," said Ellen.

"I suppose you were captured by a

chicken, were you?" said Mirror-Belle.
"Not quite so exciting, really. Still, I expect
the cure's just the same." She picked up a
bottle of bubble bath and poured nearly
all of it into the water.

"That's far too much!" shrieked Ellen.
But Mirror-Belle was too busy investigating
the cupboard on the wall to answer.

"This looks good too," she said.

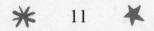

"But that's my dad's shaving cream," said Ellen.

"It's nice and frothy," said Mirror-Belle, squirting some into the bath. "And *this* looks just the job," she said, taking the cap off a tube of Minty-Zing toothpaste, which had red and green stripes.

"Nice colours," said Mirror-Belle, squeezing most of the toothpaste out into the bath.

Ellen was a bit shocked at first but then she giggled.

"Shall we put some of Luke's hair gel in too?" she asked. Ellen's big brother had started getting interested in his appearance recently and was always smoothing bright blue sticky stuff into his hair.

"Good idea," said Mirror-Belle. Ellen scooped the gel out of the tube and into the bath. That would serve Luke right for all the times he'd hogged the hairdryer.

Mirror-Belle poured in a bottle of orange-coloured shampoo and eyed the bath water thought-fully. "We still need one more ingredient," she said. "*I* know!" She picked up Mum's bottle of Blue Moon perfume and began spraying merrily.

Ellen, who had begun to enjoy herself, felt rather alarmed again. Mum only ever put a tiny bit of Blue Moon behind her ears. By now the bathroom smelt like a flower shop.

"Let's get in now," said Mirror-Belle. In another moment the two of them were up to their chests in bubbles, cream, gel and toothpaste.

"I can feel the cure working already, can't you?" said Mirror-Belle, and flipped some froth at Ellen. Ellen flipped some back, and a blob of toothpaste landed on the spot on Mirror-Belle's nose.

Ellen noticed that Mirror-Belle, like herself, had a pale mark round one of her wrists.

"We've both got watch-strap marks," she said. "Did you lose your watch like I did?"

Mirror-Belle looked at her grandly and said, "This mark isn't from a *watch*. Oh no. It's from my magic wishing bangle."

"A wishing bangle! Can you wish for anything you want?"

"Naturally," said Mirror-Belle. "And for things that other people *don't* want."

"Such as?"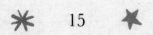

"Well, once I wished for a worm in the palace garden to grow to the size of a snake and give the gardener a fright."

"And did it?"

"Yes. The only trouble was, it didn't stop growing. It grew and grew till it took up the whole of the garden. Then we had to banish it to an island, but it *still* kept growing."

"But couldn't you just wish it small again?"

Mirror-Belle looked annoyed for a second but then her face cleared and she said, "No, because I dropped the bangle in the sea and it got swallowed by a fish. Luckily, though, I caught the fish last week."

Ellen thought of reminding her once again that she had said she was asleep

last week, but she decided not to. It would only make Mirror-Belle cross. It was more fun just to listen to her stories, even if some of them sounded a bit like fibs.

"I don't feel quite so bad about missing the dolphin display any more," she said.

"Is *that* all you're missing?" asked Mirror-Belle. "*I'm* missing the sea monster display."

The two of them played at being dolphins and sea monsters for a while, splashing a lot of water and froth out of the bath.

"Your dragon pox hasn't gone away yet," said Ellen.

"Don't be so impatient," said Mirror-Belle. "We haven't done Stage Two yet."

"What's that?"

"Get out and I'll show you," said Mirror-Belle. They both got out of the bath and Mirror-Belle picked up a roll of toilet paper. She began winding it round and round Ellen, starting with her legs and working upwards.

"I feel like an Egyptian mummy," said Ellen, laughing.

Mirror-Belle reached Ellen's face. She wound the paper round and round until Ellen couldn't see out.

"Now you have to count to a hundred," she said.

"What about you?" asked Ellen.

"We'll do me later," said Mirror-Belle.

Ellen started to count. She could hear Mirror-Belle moving about the room and from downstairs came the sound of Mrs Foster-Smith playing "The Babbling Brook". The way she played it, it sounded more like "The Crashing Ocean".

When Ellen got to about eighty she heard Mirror-Belle say something which sounded like, "Ow! Stupid old taps!"

When she got to a hundred she tried to unwind the toilet paper but it got into a tangle.

"Help me, Mirror-Belle," she said. But there was silence.

Ellen managed to tear the toilet paper away from her eyes, but Mirror-Belle was nowhere to be seen.

"Mirror-Belle! Where are you?" called Ellen. Mirror-Belle's pyjamas had disappeared as well. Could she have put them on and gone out of the room?

Ellen opened the door. Maybe Mirror-Belle had gone downstairs. Ellen was still half-wrapped in toilet paper but she didn't bother about that. She set off downstairs in search of Mirror-Belle.

When she was six stairs from the bottom, two things happened. Ellen 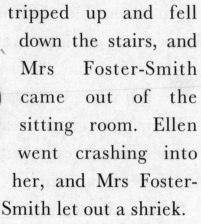 tripped up and fell down the stairs, and Mrs Foster-Smith came out of the sitting room. Ellen went crashing into her, and Mrs Foster-Smith let out a shriek.

"Ellen! What *are* you up to?" asked Mum, following Mrs Foster-Smith out of the room.

"It's Stage Two. It's all to do with dragon pox," Ellen began explaining.

"Mirror-Belle said that the cure for chicken pox was just the same. You need bubble bath and toothpaste and hair gel and . . ."

"The child's raving – she's delirious," said Mrs Foster-Smith. "I think we ought to call the doctor."

"I don't think it's that bad," said Mum.

"Go and put your pyjamas back on, Ellen, and I'll be with you in a minute. I'll see you at the same time next week then, Mrs Foster-Smith. And as I said, maybe you could try playing the pieces just a *little* more quietly."

Back in the bathroom, Ellen finished untangling herself. She had just got into her pyjamas when Mum came into the room. She looked round in horror at the empty jars and bottles and the froth everywhere.

"What a horrible mess!" she said.

"It wasn't me – not much of it, anyway. It was Mirror-Belle. She came out of the mirror."

"Oh yes, and I suppose she's gone back into it now."

Ellen looked at the mirror. It was covered in toothpasty bubbles.

"I think you're right," she said.

Mum wiped the bubbles off the mirror. Ellen looked into it. The girl she saw there *did* look like Mirror-Belle, but she moved whenever Ellen moved: it was just her own reflection.

Ellen frowned, suddenly unsure about

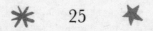

everything. She couldn't just have imagined
Mirror-Belle, could she? Her reflection
frowned back.

Mum scurried round the room, tut-
tutting and clearing up the mess. The
worst part was when she discovered how
little of her Blue Moon perfume was left.

"I know I leave you on your own a lot when I do my piano-teaching, but I *did* think you were old enough not to do things like this," she said. "You should be in bed with those chicken pox – though I must say, they do look quite a bit better. That big one on your nose seems to have disappeared!"

Then she caught sight of something in the basin and, looking surprised, picked it up.

"Look – here's your left slipper!" she said. "I'm glad it's turned up at last."

Ellen didn't say anything (that would only annoy Mum again) but she smiled to herself as she put the slipper on, because she knew whose slipper it really was.

Chapter Two

Ellen's Castle

Ellen and her mother were in one of the changing rooms of a big department store. They were supposed to be buying a dress for Ellen to wear to her grown-up cousin's wedding, but nothing seemed to fit or look right.

"That greeny-blue colour suits you," said Ellen's mum, "but it's too tight. I'll go and see if they've got a bigger size."

Ellen didn't really care *what* dress she

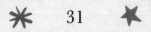

wore to the wedding. No one would be looking at her, since she hadn't been asked to be a bridesmaid – something she felt a bit cross about. She practised making her most hideous face at herself in the mirror – the one where her eyeballs rolled up and almost out of sight and her bottom lip jutted over the top one. If she did that at the wedding, people *would* look at her. But of course she'd be too shy to do it when the time came.

This time, though, the face didn't seem to be working properly. The eyeballs in the mirror rolled back to normal, the mouth went back to its ordinary shape, then opened and said, "You look just like that wicked fairy – the one who pricked my finger."

"Mirror-Belle!" exclaimed Ellen. "What are you doing here?"

Mirror-Belle stepped out of the mirror. She was wearing a too-tight, greeny-blue dress just like the one Ellen had on.

"I see you've moved house," she said, looking around her.

"This isn't a house, it's a shop," said Ellen, but Mirror-Belle wasn't listening. She had picked up Ellen's coat from the floor where it was lying inside out, and was putting it on that way, so that the tartan lining was on the outside.

"Not bad," she said, looking at her reflection. Then, "Come on, let's see what your cook has made for lunch." And she walked out of the changing room.

"No! Stop!" cried Ellen. "Give me back my coat!" She ran after Mirror-Belle, who was merrily weaving her way around the rails and stands of clothes.

"You *have* got a lot of clothes," she said when Ellen caught up with her. "Almost as

many as me, though not such beautiful ones, of course. I don't suppose you've got a ballgown made of rose petals stitched together with spider's thread, have you?"

"No, I haven't," said Ellen. "But I don't think I'd want one. Wouldn't the rose petals shrivel up and die?"

Mirror-Belle thought for a moment and then said, "No, they've been dipped in a magic fountain which keeps them fresh forever."

By this stage they had reached the escalator. Mirror-Belle hopped on to it.

"This is fun," she said. "Does it go down to the dungeons?"

"No," said Ellen, riding down beside her. "It goes down to the food department."

"The banqueting hall, do you mean?" asked Mirror-Belle. "Oh good, I'm starving."

She skipped off the escalator. They were in the fruit and vegetable section of the food department. Mirror-Belle picked up a potato and put it down again in disgust.

"It's *raw!*" she said. "How does your cook expect us to eat that?" She inspected the cabbages and cauliflowers. "What sort of banquet is *this* supposed to be?" she asked. "None of the food is cooked at all."

"It's not *supposed* to be cooked – people take it home to cook," Ellen tried to

explain. "Look, Mirror-Belle, do give me back my raincoat – I must get back to Mum."

"These apples look all right," said Mirror-Belle, picking one up and taking a large bite out of it. She picked up another one and did the same. "With green and red apples like these I only ever bite the green side," she explained. "You can't be too careful – there could be a wicked queen going round putting poison into the red sides. Look what happened to my friend Snow White." She took a bite out of another apple.

Just then a shop assistant came up. "Stop eating the fruit," she said to Mirror-Belle.

"Start cooking the vegetables!" Mirror-Belle said back to her.

The shop assistant looked startled, and asked Mirror-Belle where her mum or dad was.

"Sitting on their thrones, I expect," said Mirror-Belle. "Come on, Ellen, let's go and play in your bedroom." She grabbed Ellen's hand and pulled her into a lift.

"Does this go up to the battlements?" she asked as the doors closed.

"No," said Ellen. "You seem to think this is some kind of castle but it's not, it's a—"

"Ah, *here's* your bedroom," said Mirror-Belle as the lift doors opened on the second floor. They were in the furniture department. Mirror-Belle darted past some armchairs and sofas to an area full of beds and mattresses. She flung herself down on a double bed and almost immediately sprang off it again.

"I hope you don't sleep on *that* one," she said. "I certainly couldn't sleep a wink on it."

"No, I don't," said Ellen. "This isn't my—"

"Good," said Mirror-Belle, "because there's a pea under the mattress."

"How do you know?"

"We princesses can always tell," said Mirror-Belle, and she flopped down on to another bed. "Ugh!" she said. "There's a baked bean under this one – horribly lumpy. Lie down and maybe you'll be able to feel it too."

Ellen giggled. She looked around. There wasn't a shop assistant in sight. She lay down on the bed next to Mirror-Belle. It felt wonderfully springy and comfortable.

"I can't feel anything," she said.

"That must be because you're not a princess," said Mirror-Belle. "Ordinary people have to bounce to detect peas and beans under mattresses. Like this." She got to her feet and began to jump up and down on the bed.

"Come on!" she said.

Ellen looked around again. There were still no shop assistants to be seen. She joined Mirror-Belle and soon the two of them were bouncing about on the bed, making the springs of the mattress twang.

"This is nearly as good as the school trampoline," said Ellen breathlessly.

"It's not as good as the *palace* trampoline," said Mirror-Belle. "I once bounced right up into the clouds from that."

"Did you come down all right?"

"No, I didn't," said Mirror-Belle. "The North Wind saw me up there and swept me away to the land of ice."

"What happened then?"

But Ellen never found out because at that moment an angry-looking shop assistant came towards them.

"Quick! Let's run!" Ellen said. But Mirror-Belle had a different idea. She jumped off the bed and

* 43

advanced towards the assistant as angrily as he was advancing towards them.

"Ah, there you are at last!" she said, before he had a chance to speak. "I want to complain about the state of this bedroom. Peas and beans under all the mattresses – it's disgraceful! Set to work removing them immediately or you'll be fired from the castle!" And with that she linked her arm in Ellen's, turned and strode off towards the escalator. The shop assistant was left gawping as they sailed up to the toy department.

"So this is your playroom, is it?" asked Mirror-Belle.

Ellen tried to explain that they weren't *her* toys, but Mirror-Belle was already emptying the pieces of a jigsaw puzzle out on to the floor.

"Too much sky in this one," she said, and moved on.

"Aren't you going to clear it up?" asked Ellen.

"What, and let your lazy servants get even lazier? Certainly not."

Mirror-Belle continued down the aisle of toys, emptying out various boxes, not satisfied till she reached a shelf full of cuddly toys. There were teddies and rabbits, puppies and monkeys, but Mirror-Belle picked up a furry green frog and kissed it on the nose.

"Why are you doing that?" asked Ellen.

"I'm turning him into a prince," said Mirror-Belle. "Princesses can do that, you know."

"Even *furry* frogs?"

"Yes, they just turn into furry princes, that's all. This one seems to want to stay a frog, though," said Mirror-Belle. "All right, you silly creature, away you leap," and she threw the frog across the shop and turned her attention to a teddy.

"I've never tried it on a bear," she said.

But Ellen had noticed a man coming towards them from about where the frog must have landed. He looked even crosser than the bed man had done. She tugged at Mirror-Belle's sleeve in alarm, but Mirror-Belle looked delighted to see the man.

"Don't you see, it's the *prince*," she said. "He doesn't look a very nice prince, mind you," she went on as the man drew closer. "You're not very furry either," as he came right up to them, "unless you count your funny woolly moustache."

"What do you think you're doing?" the man asked.

"Aren't you going to say thank you?" Mirror-Belle said to him.

"What, for throwing toys around?"

"No, for breaking the spell, of course," said Mirror-Belle. "Though if I'd known what a bad-tempered prince you'd turn out to be I wouldn't have bothered. Can't say I blame that witch for turning you into a frog in the first place. Come on, Ellen!"

She turned and walked briskly away, calling over her shoulder, "And if you think you're going to marry me you've got another think coming."

The man stood rooted to the spot for a few moments, too

astounded to follow them. By the time he did, Mirror-Belle and Ellen had dived into a lift. Mirror-Belle pressed the top button.

"Perhaps *this*'ll take us to the battlements at last," she said.

"It says 'Offices Only'," said Ellen.

When they got out they were in a corridor with a few doors leading off it. One of the doors was ajar and Ellen could hear a familiar voice coming from it.

"I only went out for a couple of minutes to look for another dress, and when I got back she'd gone."

Ellen couldn't bear to hear Mum sounding so upset.

"Come with me," she said to Mirror-Belle and ran into the room. Her mother was there with another lady.

"Oh *there* you are, darling," said Mum, hugging her. "Where *have* you been?"

"With Mirror-Belle. She took my coat so I had to follow her," said Ellen. "She's just outside." She took her mother's hand and pulled her into the corridor. There was no one there.

"You didn't mention another little girl," said the shop lady to Mum.

"There isn't one really – it's just my daughter's imaginary friend."

"She's not imaginary, she's real," Ellen protested.

The light outside the lift showed that it was still on the top floor. "She must be in here," said Ellen, pressing the button.

The doors opened. Apart from a crumpled raincoat with a tartan lining lying on the floor, the lift was empty. Where on earth was Princess Mirror-Belle?

It was only then that Ellen noticed something which she should have spotted before.

The walls of the lift were covered in mirrors.

Princess Mirror-Belle had disappeared!

Chapter Three

Snow White and the Eight Dwarfs

Ellen's big brother Luke was singing again.

"Seven little hats on seven little heads. Seven little pillows on seven little beds," he sang, standing on a ladder and dabbing paint on to the branches of a canvas tree. A blob of paint landed on Ellen's hand. She was squatting on the stage, painting the tree trunk.

Ellen sighed heavily – more because

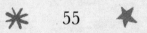

of the song than the blob of paint. Luke had been singing the seven dwarfs' song almost non-stop ever since he'd joined the local drama group and got a part in the Christmas pantomime.

"Seven pairs of trousers on fourteen little legs," he sang now.

"No one could call *your* legs little," said Ellen. "You should be acting a giant, not a dwarf."

"There aren't any giants in *Snow White*, dumbo," said Luke. "Anyway, I told you, we all walk about on our knees."

"So that Sally Hart can pat you on the head," said Ellen. She knew that Luke was keen on Sally Hart. In fact, she guessed that he was only in the pantomime because Sally was acting Snow White.

Luke blushed but all he said was, "Shut up or I won't get you a ticket for tonight."

The first performance of *Snow White* was that evening, and at the last minute the director had decided that the forest needed a couple of extra trees. Luke had volunteered to go and paint them, and Mum had persuaded him to take Ellen along.

Although Ellen was too shy to want to be in the play, it was fun being in the theatre in front of all the rows of empty seats. But Luke wouldn't let her have a go on the ladder, and soon she had painted the bottom of the two tree trunks.

Luke was getting quite carried away with the leaves and acorns, still singing the annoying song all the time. He didn't seem to notice when Ellen wandered off to explore the theatre. She opened a door in a narrow passageway behind the stage.

The room was dark and Ellen switched on the light – or rather, the lights: there was a whole row of bulbs, all shining brightly above a long mirror. This must be one of the dressing rooms.

Some beards were hanging up on a row of hooks. Ellen guessed they belonged to the seven dwarfs. She unhooked one and tried it on. It was quite tickly.

"Seven little beards on seven little chins," she sang into the mirror.

"And seven mouldy cauliflowers in seven smelly bins," her reflection sang back at her.

But of course it wasn't her reflection. It was Princess Mirror-Belle.

Quickly, Ellen turned her back, hoping

that Mirror-Belle would stay in the mirror.
Mirror-Belle was the last person she
wanted to see just now. Their adventures
together always seemed to land Ellen in
trouble.

But it was too late. Mirror-Belle had
climbed out of the mirror and was tapping
Ellen on the shoulder.

"Let's have a look at your beard," she said, and then, as Ellen turned round, "I'd shave it off if I were you – it doesn't suit you."

"It's only a play one," said Ellen. "Anyway, you've got one too."

"I know." Mirror-Belle sighed. "The hairdresser said the wrong spell and I ended up with a beard instead of short hair."

"Couldn't the hairdresser use scissors instead of spells?" asked Ellen.

"Good heavens no," said Mirror-Belle. "An ordinary one could, maybe, but this is the *palace* hairdresser we're talking about."

She turned to a rail of costumes, pulled a robin outfit off its hanger and held it up against herself.

"Put that back!" cried Ellen, and then, "You'll get it all painty!"

They both looked at Mirror-Belle's left hand, which had paint on it, just like Ellen's right one.

"Have you been painting trees too?" Ellen asked.

"No, of course not." Mirror-Belle looked thoughtful as she hung the robin costume back on the rail. Then, "No – trees have been painting *me*," she said.

Ellen couldn't help laughing. "How can they do *that*?" she asked.

"Not *all* trees can do it," replied Mirror-Belle. "Just the ones in the magic forest. They bend down their branches and dip them into the muddy lake and paint anyone who comes past."

"How strange," said Ellen.

"I don't think it's so strange as people painting trees, which is what you say you've been doing," said Mirror-Belle.

"They're not real trees," Ellen explained. "They're for a play."

Mirror-Belle looked quite interested. "Can I help?" she asked.

"No, you certainly can't," said Ellen, horrified, but Mirror-Belle wasn't put off.

"What sort of trees are they?" she asked. "I'm very good at painting bananas. And pineapples."

"Pineapples don't grow on trees, and anyway—" but Ellen broke off because she heard the stage door bang.

"Ellen! Where are you?" came Luke's voice.

"I'm coming!" Ellen yelled. Then she hissed to Mirror-Belle, "Get back into the mirror! Don't mess about with the costumes! And *stay away from the trees*!"

That evening Ellen was back in the theatre, sitting in the audience next to Mum and Dad. *Snow White* was about to start.

Mum squeezed Ellen's hand. "You look nervous," she said. "Don't worry – I'm sure Luke will be fine."

But it wasn't Luke that Ellen was nervous about – it was Mirror-Belle. What had she been up to in the empty theatre all afternoon? Ellen was terrified that when the curtain went up, the trees would be covered in tropical fruit and the costumes would be covered in paint.

The curtain went up. There were no bananas or pineapples to be seen. The forest looked beautiful. Dad leaned across Mum's seat and whispered, "Very well-painted trees, Ellen."

Sally Hart – or rather, Snow White – looked beautiful too, with her black

hair, big eyes and rosy
cheeks. Over her arm
she carried a basket,
and she fed
breadcrumbs to a
chorus of hungry
robins. None of
them seemed
to have paint on
their costumes.

Ellen breathed a sigh of relief. Everything
was all right after all! Mirror-Belle must
have gone back into the dressing-room
mirror.

A palace scene came next. When the
wicked Queen looked into her magic
mirror and asked,

"Mirror, mirror on the wall,

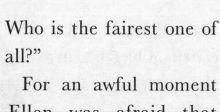

Who is the fairest one of all?"

For an awful moment Ellen was afraid that Mirror-Belle might come leaping out of the mirror, shouting "I am!" But of course she could only do that if it was *Ellen* looking into the mirror. Stop being so jumpy, Ellen told herself – Mirror-Belle is safely back in her own world.

When the scene changed to the dwarfs' cottage, Mum gave Ellen a nudge. Soon Luke would be coming on stage!

And yes, now Snow White was asleep in one of the beds, and here came the dwarfs, shuffling in through the cottage door. Ellen knew that they were walking on their knees but the costumes were so good, with shoes stitched on to the front of the baggy trousers, that you couldn't really tell.

Luke was acting the bossiest dwarf – Typical, Ellen thought. He told the others to hang up their jackets and set the table. Then they started to dance around and sing the song that Ellen was so tired of hearing.

"Seven little jackets on seven little pegs. Seven little eggcups, and seven little eggs."

But something was wrong. One of the dwarfs was singing much louder than the others, and not getting all the words right. When the other dwarfs stopped singing and started to tap out the tune on

the table, the dwarf with the loud voice carried on:

"Seven stupid people who don't know how to count. Can't they see that seven is not the right amount?"

The audience laughed as they realised that there were *eight* dwarfs and not seven. But Ellen didn't laugh. Dwarf number eight had to be Mirror-Belle, and there was bound to be serious trouble ahead.

Up on the stage, Luke looked furious. He stopped tapping the table and started chasing Mirror-Belle round the room. He was trying to chase her out of the door but she kept dodging him as she carried on singing:

"Eight little spoons and eight little bowls.

Sixteen little woolly socks with sixteen great big holes."

Ellen felt like shouting, or throwing something, or rushing on to the stage herself and dragging Mirror-Belle off. But that would just make things worse. All she could do was to watch in horror.

In the end, Luke gave up the chase. With one last glare at Mirror-Belle he strode over to the bed where Snow White was sleeping. His cross expression changed to one of adoration when Snow White woke up and sang a song.

"Will you stay with us?" Luke begged

her when the song had finished.

"Yes, do stay and look after us," said another dwarf.

"We need someone to comb our beards."

"And wash our clothes."

"And shine our shoes."

"And cook our meals."

"And clean our house."

All the dwarfs except Mirror-Belle were chiming in.

"There's nothing I'd like better!" exclaimed Snow White.

Mirror-Belle turned on her. "You must be joking," she said angrily. "You shouldn't be doing things like that – you're a *princess*! You should be bossing *them* about, not the other way round."

The audience laughed – except for Ellen – and Snow White's mouth fell open. Ellen felt sorry for her: she obviously didn't know what to say. But Luke came to the rescue.

"Be quiet!" he ordered Mirror-Belle. "You don't know anything about princesses."

"Of course I do – I *am* one!" Mirror-Belle retorted. "I'm just in disguise as a dwarf. I thought Snow White might need some protection against that horrible Queen. I'm pretty sure she's going to be along soon with a tray of poisoned apples, and—"

"Shut up, you're spoiling the story!" hissed Luke, and put a hand over Mirror-

Belle's mouth. Snow White looked at him in admiration. Luke made a sign to someone offstage, and a second later the curtain came down. It was the end of the first half.

"Isn't Luke good?" said Mum in the interval. "He never told us he had such a big part."

"That little girl playing the extra dwarf is a hoot, isn't she?" said Dad. "She sounds a bit like you, Ellen. Who is she?"

"I don't know," muttered Ellen. It was no use mentioning Mirror-Belle to her

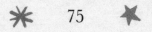

parents, who just thought she was an imaginary friend. Ellen licked her ice cream but she was too worried to enjoy it properly. What would Mirror-Belle get up to in the second half of the show?

The curtain went up again. Snow White was sweeping the dwarfs' cottage. Ellen was relieved that there was no sign of Mirror-Belle. She must have gone off to work with the other dwarfs.

The wicked Queen appeared at the cottage window. She looked quite different – like an old woman – as she held out a tray of apples and offered one to Snow White.

"The dwarfs made me promise not to buy anything from a stranger," said Snow White.

"There's no need to buy," replied the disguised Queen. "Just open the window, and I'll give you one!"

Snow White opened the window and took an apple in her hand. She still looked doubtful.

"Don't you trust me?" asked the Queen. "Look, I'll take a bite out of it myself first to prove that it's all right." She did this and handed the apple back to Snow White.

Snow White had just opened her mouth when a voice cried, "Stop!" and a second figure appeared at the cottage window. Oh no! It was Mirror-Belle.

"Stop! Don't you realise, she took that bite out of the green half of the apple. It's the red half that's poisoned!" she warned Snow White.

Snow White took no notice and was about to bite into the apple when Mirror-Belle snatched it from her. She snatched the tray of apples from the Queen too. The next moment she had burst in through the cottage door, pursued by the Queen.

Some steps led down from the stage into the audience, and Mirror-Belle ran down them. She ran through the audience, the Queen hot on her heels.

When Mirror-Belle reached Ellen's seat she whispered, "Here, take this!" and thrust the tray of apples on to Ellen's lap. Ellen didn't know what to do, but was saved from doing anything by the Queen, who snatched the tray back. Mirror-Belle grabbed it from her again and ran on.

Meanwhile, Snow White, who had run off the back of the stage, reappeared holding Luke's hand and followed by the other dwarfs. They joined in the chase, round and round the audience and back on to the stage. Luke overtook the others. He caught Mirror-Belle by the shoulders and shook her.

"Give back those apples!" he ordered.

"What! Do you *want* Snow White to be poisoned?" protested Mirror-Belle. "Some friend you are!"

"Who is she, anyway?" asked Snow White – except that she didn't sound like Snow White any more, she sounded like Sally Hart.

"I don't know but we'll soon find out!" said Luke – sounding like Luke and not a dwarf – and he ripped Mirror-Belle's beard off.

"Ellen, it's you!" he exclaimed.

"Oh no I'm not!" said Mirror-Belle. "Your sister Ellen is in the audience – there, look!" She pointed, and to Ellen's embarrassment not only Luke but everyone else on the stage and in the audience was looking at her.

Not for long, though. Soon all eyes

were back on Mirror-Belle, who was throwing apples into the audience.

"Don't eat them, *and don't give them back*!" she ordered.

Just then a man in a suit came on to the stage. Ellen recognised him as Mr Turnbull, the director. He strode up to Mirror-Belle.

"I don't know who you are or where you come from, but you'd better go back there before I call the police!" he said.

"Don't worry, I will!" said Mirror-Belle. Mr Turnbull made a grab for her but she dodged him and ran out through the cottage door. Mr Turnbull and all the actors followed her, and Ellen heard the Queen shout, "Oh no! She's got my mirror now!"

A moment later, Mirror-Belle was climbing back into the cottage through the open window, clutching the Queen's mirror. She scuttled into the dwarfs' cupboard just as everyone else came charging back in through the door.

"Where is she?" asked Mr Turnbull, with his back to the cupboard. Mirror-Belle popped her head out.

"She's behind you!" yelled the audience. Mr Turnbull turned round but now the cupboard door was shut.

"Oh no she's not!" said Mr Turnbull.

"OH YES SHE IS!" the audience shouted back.

Snow White opened the cupboard door and peered in.

"Is she there?" asked Mr Turnbull.

"I don't think so," said Snow White. She picked up her broom and swept around inside, just to make sure. "What's this?" she asked, as she swept an object out of the cupboard.

"It's my magic mirror!" said the Queen. "So she must have been here."

"Well, she's gone now, thank goodness," said Mr Turnbull. He turned to face the audience.

"I'm sorry about all this, ladies and gentlemen," he said. "Anyone who wants their money back can ask at the box office. But now, on with the show!"

"Seven little cups and seven little plates," sang Mum next day, as she served up Ellen's lunch. Luke was having a lie-in.

"Oh, Mum, don't *you* start!"

"Sorry. Wasn't Luke brilliant last night?

I can't wait to show him the piece in the paper."

"Let's have a look."

Mum passed Ellen the paper, and this is what she read:

"The Pinkerton Players' performance of *Snow White* last night was a comic triumph. The hilarious chase scene was hugely enjoyable, and so was the entertaining scene in which the director pretended to offer the audience their money back.

"All the cast gave excellent performances, especially Sally Hart as Snow White and Luke Page as the bossy dwarf, but the real star of the show was the child who played the Eighth Dwarf. Sadly, she was not present at the curtain call. Perhaps she was too young to stay up so late.

"I have only one criticism of the show. Why did this child star's name not appear in the programme? Everyone wants to know who she is, and everyone wants to see more of her."

Yes, thought Ellen. Everyone except me.

About the Author and Illustrator

Julia Donaldson is one of the UK's most popular children's writers. Her award-winning books include *What the Ladybird Heard, The Snail and the Whale* and *The Gruffalo.* She has also written many children's plays and songs, and her sell-out shows based on her books and songs are a huge success. She was the Children's Laureate from 2011 to 2013, campaigning for libraries and for deaf children, and creating a website for teachers called picturebookplays.co.uk. Julia and her husband Malcolm divide their time between Sussex and Edinburgh. You can find out more about Julia at www.juliadonaldson.co.uk.

Lydia Monks studied Illustration at Kingston University, graduating in 1994 with a first-class degree. She is a former winner of the Smarties Bronze Award for *I Wish I Were a Dog* and has illustrated many books by Julia Donaldson. Her illustrations have been widely admired.

Also available

For younger readers